W9-BOM-295

Dear Parents:

Congratulations! Your child is taking the first steps on an exciting journey. The destination? Independent reading!

STEP INTO READING® will help your child get there. The program offers five steps to reading success. Each step includes fun stories and colorful art or photographs. In addition to original fiction and books with favorite characters, there are Step into Reading Non-Fiction Readers, Phonics Readers and Boxed Sets, Sticker Readers, and Comic Readers—a complete literacy program with something to interest every child.

Learning to Read, Step by Step!

Ready to Read   Preschool–Kindergarten
• big type and easy words • rhyme and rhythm • picture clues
For children who know the alphabet and are eager to begin reading.

Reading with Help   Preschool–Grade 1
• basic vocabulary • short sentences • simple stories
For children who recognize familiar words and sound out new words with help.

Reading on Your Own   Grades 1–3
• engaging characters • easy-to-follow plots • popular topics
For children who are ready to read on their own.

Reading Paragraphs   Grades 2–3
• challenging vocabulary • short paragraphs • exciting stories
For newly independent readers who read simple sentences with confidence.

Ready for Chapters   Grades 2–4
• chapters • longer paragraphs • full-color art
For children who want to take the plunge into chapter books but still like colorful pictures.

STEP INTO READING® is designed to give every child a successful reading experience. The grade levels are only guides; children will progress through the steps at their own speed, developing confidence in their reading.

Remember, a lifetime love of reading starts with a single step!

Step into Reading, Random House, and the Random House colophon are registered trademarks
of Penguin Random House LLC.

Visit us on the Web!
StepIntoReading.com
rhcbooks.com

Educators and librarians, for a variety of teaching tools, visit us at RHTeachersLibrarians.com

ISBN 978-0-7364-3987-9 (trade) — ISBN 978-0-7364-8277-6 (lib. bdg.)
ISBN 978-0-7364-3988-6 (ebook)

Printed in the United States of America   10 9 8 7 6 5 4 3 2

Disney · PIXAR

TOY STORY 4

MADE TO PLAY!

by Natasha Bouchard

illustrated by the Disney Storybook Art Team

Random House 🏠 New York

It is Bonnie's
first day of school.
She is nervous.

Woody helps Bonnie.

He sneaks art supplies

to her table.

Bonnie makes Forky.

He is her

new favorite toy!

Forky meets
Bonnie's other toys.
Forky does not think
he is a toy.
He thinks he belongs
in the trash.

Bonnie takes her toys
on a family road trip.
Forky runs away!

Woody finds him.
He tells Forky
that he is special
to Bonnie.

Woody sees

Bo Peep's lamp

in a store window!

Bo Peep is
Woody's old friend.
Woody and Forky go
inside to find her.

They meet Gabby Gabby.

She is a broken doll.

She wants to be fixed.

Gabby Gabby says
she can help
them find Bo.

Gabby Gabby wants
Woody's voice box.
Then a kid will want her.

Woody gets away.

Forky is caught!

He is trapped

in the store.

Woody finds Bo Peep
and her sheep.

They will help Woody
get Forky back.

Woody and Bo find
more friends to help
rescue Forky.
They sneak back
into the store.

Duke Caboom lives
in the store.
He will help, too.

The toys
have a plan.
But their plan
does not work!
Dragon the cat
stops them.

Woody gives
Gabby Gabby
his voice box.
She lets Forky go.

The toys find a kid
for Gabby Gabby.

Woody is glad
to have the help
of his friends!

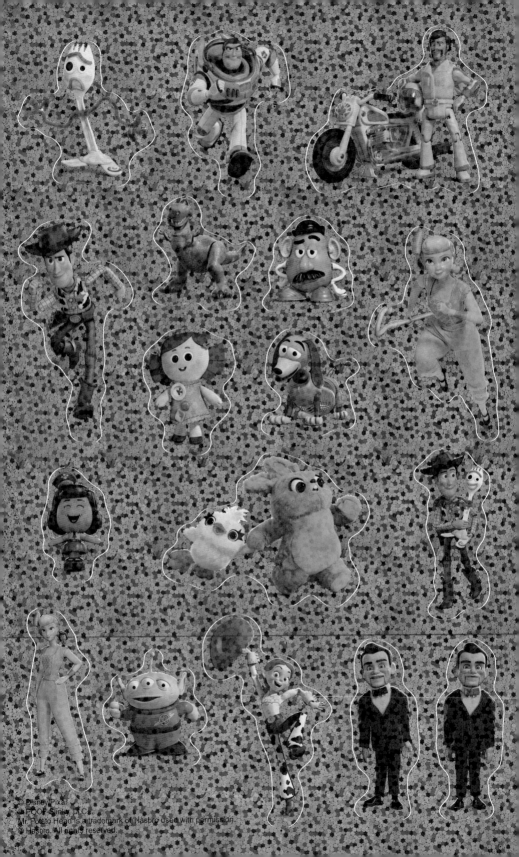